DANCE

MODERN *Dance*

by Wendy Garofoli

Consultant: Michele Rusinko
Professor of Dance, Gustavus Adolphus College
St. Peter, Minnesota

Capstone *press*®

Mankato, Minnesota

Snap Books are published by Capstone Press,
151 Good Counsel Drive, P.O. Box 669, Mankato, Minnesota 56002.
www.capstonepress.com

Library of Congress Cataloging-in-Publication Data
Garofoli, Wendy.
Modern dance / by Wendy Garofoli.
p. cm. — (Snap books. Dance)
Summary: "Describes modern dance, including history and basic
steps" — Provided by publisher.
Includes bibliographical references and index.
ISBN-13: 978-1-4296-1353-8 (hardcover)
ISBN-10: 1-4296-1353-X (hardcover)
1. Modern dance — Juvenile literature. I. Title. II. Series.
GV1783.G27 2008
792.8 — dc22   2007024745

Editor: Jennifer Besel

Designer: Veronica Bianchini

Photo Researcher: Jo Miller

Photo Credits: All photos by Capstone Press/Karon Dubke, except:
AP Images/Wally Santana, 26–27
Corbis/Bettmann, 8 (bottom); Robble Jack, 6
Courtesy of the author Wendy Garofoli, 32
Getty Images Inc./Hulton Archive, 7, 8 (top); Stone+/PM Images, 5; Time & Life Pictures/Pix Inc./Jerry Cooke, 9

Acknowledgements:
Capstone Press would like to thank Kerry Casserly and the dancers at the Lundstrum Center for the Performing Arts
in Minneapolis, Minnesota, for their assistance preparing this book.

Table of Contents

Chapter One

MEANINGFUL MOVEMENTS

It's the study of how the body moves. It's the exploration of shapes the body can make. It's the development of rhythm and timing. What is it? It's modern dance.

Modern dancers use their bodies and the space around them to express themselves. In modern dance pieces, you'll see dancers move in jumps, leaps, turns, and falls. They will make shapes with their bodies. They'll move fast and slow, back and forth, up and down. And they might tell you a story through dance.

How it Started

When you hear the word modern, you probably think of something that is happening right now. And modern dance is just that. Dancers are always experimenting with new movements. But modern dance as an art form has been around for almost 100 years.

Isadora Duncan has been called a genius for developing a new dance style. In the early 1900s, ballet was the only studied form of dance. But Duncan wanted a dance that had more freedom of movement. Instead of wearing a tutu and pointe shoes, she danced barefoot and wore a short Greek tunic. She skipped and let her arms fall freely to her sides. Duncan performed as a way to express herself. And in doing so, she influenced generations of modern dancers to come.

Modern dance is an expressive art. The art has changed over time, thanks to some amazing dancers. Mary Wigman's style was filled with emotion and drama. Ruth St. Denis and Ted Shawn formed Denishawn, a school and dance company. At Denishawn, students learned new movements that were loosely based on other world dance forms. Alvin Ailey combined elements of jazz and African dance with modern. And the list goes on. Modern dance is about being an individual. So any modern dancer, even you, influences the form in some way.

Spotlight

Martha Graham is considered the mother of modern dance. Graham's movement style featured sharp, angular arms. She performed contractions, where she curved her spine into a "C" shape. Graham's dances were intense and experimental. Her work as a dancer and choreographer, which spanned from the 1920s to her death in 1991, was a major influence on modern dance. Graham's technique is often taught in dance studios even today.

FIRST THINGS FIRST

Before you begin expressing yourself, you'll have to get ready. Modern dance classes are all different, depending on the teacher.

It might be a good idea to sit in on a couple of classes to get a feel for the teacher's technique. A great teacher is the key to success. You'll want a teacher who corrects your movements when your motion isn't quite right.

What to Wear

Before you start, check with your instructor about the dress code. Most of the time, you'll wear knit pants and a tank top. Make sure that your clothes are snug on your body. A baggy T-shirt hides your body. Your teacher won't be able to see you move.

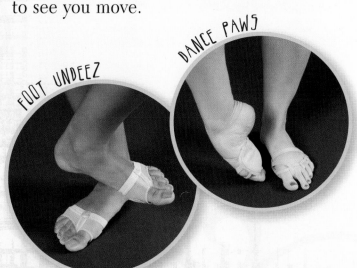

FOOT UNDEEZ

DANCE PAWS

Modern dancers perform barefoot. So you won't need any shoes. But when you first start, blisters on your feet could be a problem. You might want to buy coverings called Dance Paws or Foot Undeez. They will protect the balls of your feet while you're learning.

Warm Up

It's important to warm up your body before dance class. Your body will need to twist and turn to get into the right positions. If your body isn't loosened up, you could get hurt. Here are a couple good stretches to get those muscles warmed up and ready to go.

Swings:

Swings are a good move to start with. Start with your feet slightly apart and toes facing forward. Stretch your arms over your head. Then swing them down as you bend your knees. When you straighten your knees back up, bring your arms up too.

Butterfly Stretch:

The butterfly stretch is good for the torso and back. Sit down on the floor, putting the soles of your feet together. Hold your ankles for support and slowly bend your spine, so your head touches your toes. Stay there for a bit, then roll back up. You can also stretch your sides in this position too. Instead of rolling forward, lean your body to the right. Rest your right elbow on the floor. Reach your left arm up over your head. Just reverse this to stretch the other side.

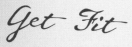
Get Fit

Many modern dancers also study Pilates or yoga to support their dance training. Both of these activities help your body prepare to move in unique ways. Pilates helps to strengthen your center, increase flexibility, and tone muscles. Yoga uses meditation and difficult body positions to achieve overall fitness. You can take Pilates or yoga at a gym or studio, or you can buy a DVD and do it at home.

DANCE EXPLORATION

Modern dance has been influenced by ballet, jazz, and other forms of dance. You might find that some modern dance teachers use ballet terms, like plié or battement tendo.

But even though the name is the same, the move could be different. Need an example? In ballet, dancers usually dance with their legs rotated out from the hip. But in modern dance, you could rotate your legs out or keep your feet pointed forward. It's up to you!

Modern dance is often performed to slow, rhythmic music. But it doesn't have to be! Modern dance is all about expression. That might mean dancing to music from the Beach Boys or Pink. Some modern dancers perform while poetry is read. Others even dance to no music at all. Be creative in your music choices and let your movements do the talking.

Body Language

Modern dance movements are like a language. Dancers can speak through their bodies. That might be a strange idea, but it's true. Imagine a dancer who wraps her arms around her stomach and curls into a ball. Could that movement express pain? Now think of a dancer leaping through the air. Maybe she's showing freedom or happiness.

Just as a frown tells someone you're mad, modern dance can be a form of communication.

Modern dancers also explore how their bodies move through the space around them. They might roll on the floor, jump into the air, or spin across the stage.

Unlike many forms of dance, modern allows dancers to move around on the floor. By using the floor, dancers are able to use the lowest spaces around them. The plank pose is one movement you could try. The plank is basically a push-up position. With your palms and toes on the floor, keep your elbows locked and your stomach tucked in. Your feet should be together and your body should be in a straight line from head to toe. For a twist on this move, try facing your head up to the ceiling.

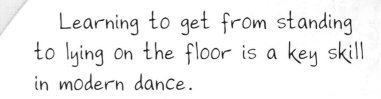

Learning to get from standing to lying on the floor is a key skill in modern dance.

The side fall is a great way to get down to the ground. Rise up on your toes and reach your arms up and to the right. Bend your right knee and slide your left leg behind it. As you bend lower to the floor, bring your arms across your body. Sit with your left leg on the ground and slide your arms out to the left. You land with both arms and legs in a straight line on the ground.

1

2

3

4

Modern dancers also try to use the space above them. That's why a modern dance piece might have lots of leaps and jumps. A tuck is a simple and fun jump to add to any performance. For a tuck, jump into the air and bend both your knees. Make sure you land with your feet together and your knees bent.

> You can do almost anything you want when it comes to jumps and leaps in modern dance. A split leap is a fun way to move your body. As you leap into the air, extend your right leg forward. Kick your left leg back behind you. You'll land on your right leg, with your knee bent. Do what feels natural with your arms. Bring them overhead or let them lift out to your sides.

A pike is another move that could be used to explore the highest spaces. Start with your knees bent and your feet together. This time when you jump, keep your legs together and straight. When you're in the air, bend your body at the waist and reach your arms toward your feet. The tricky part is landing. You'll want to land with your feet together without stumbling.

Chapter Four

MODERN MARVELS

Other than taking a class, how can you see modern dance? Check out a nearby college. Many colleges across the country have programs that emphasize modern dance.

The departments usually have performances that are open to the public. Catch one of these concerts to see how students are expressing themselves.

College dance departments often hold summer dance camps for students too. These classes are a great way to meet other modern dancers and to improve your technique.

Professional modern dance companies also tour and perform around the world. Companies like Alvin Ailey, Paul Taylor Dance Company, and Martha Graham Dance Company perform in concert halls. These companies sometimes perform in local community theaters too. Modern is the most popular dance form in the professional dance world. If you look, you're sure to find some inspiring performances.

No matter where you go or who you watch, you'll never see two identical modern dance pieces. Dancers express themselves with different facial expressions and body movements. The way they show emotion is entirely unique. And it will be the same for you. The more you study, the more you'll understand how expressive movement can be. You'll discover how to communicate emotion through a simple movement. You'll learn to speak through dance. So what are you waiting for? Get out there and express yourself!

Glossary

contraction (kuhn-TRAK-shun) — a shortening of a muscle

express (ek-SPRESS) — to show how you feel or think by doing something

Pilates (pi-LAH-teez) — an exercise program that helps tone muscles and strengthen the body's center

rhythm (RITH-uhm) — a regular beat in music, poetry, or dance

timing (TIME-ing) — to choose the moment to do something

Fast Facts

Actress Claire Danes is a modern dancer. She still performs when she's not filming movies.

Isadora Duncan called her style of dancing "free dance." Her style was so personal that it could not really be taught. That's why you won't see dance studios teaching her technique.

Read More

Anderson, Janet. *Modern Dance.* World of Dance. Philadelphia: Chelsea House, 2004.

Chryssicas, Mary Kaye. *Breathe: Yoga for Teens.* New York: DK Publishers, 2007.

Kessel, Kristin. *Martha Graham.* The Library of American Choreographers. New York: Rosen, 2006.

Internet Sites

FactHound offers a safe, fun way to find Internet sites related to this book. All of the sites on FactHound have been researched by our staff.

Here's how:

1. Visit *www.facthound.com*

2. Choose your grade level.

3. Type in this book ID **142961353X** for age-appropriate sites. You may also browse subjects by clicking on letters, or by clicking on pictures and words.

4. Click on the **Fetch It** button.

Facthound will fetch the best sites for you!

About the Author

Wendy Garofoli is a writer for *Dance Magazine*, *Dance Spirit*, *Cheer Biz News*, and *Dance Retailer News*. She studied modern at Peridance Center and Dance New Amsterdam in New York City. In addition to writing, Wendy also choreographs, teaches, and judges dance competitions.

INDEX